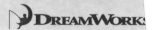

THE CROODS

SUPER SEARCH

PICTURE PUZZLES, MAZES, AND MORE

written by Bill Scollon

Reader's Digest
Children's Books

New York, New York • Montréal, Québec • Bath, United Kingdom

FAMILY GATHERING

The Croods and Guy have gathered in the jungle to figure out their next move. See if you can figure out where all the things in the box are hiding in the picture. There are several of each—find them all!

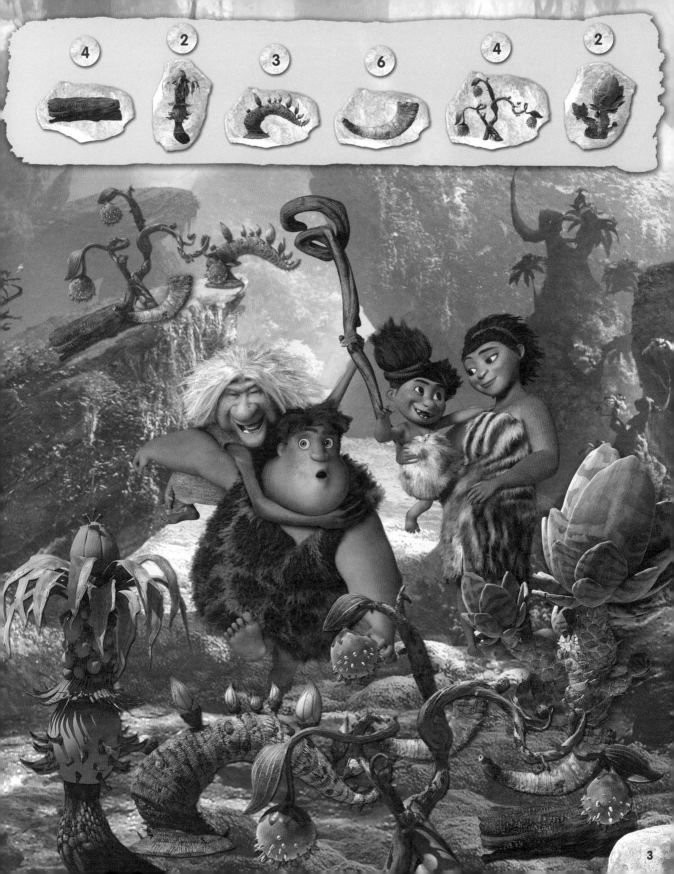

4 2 3 6 4 2

LOST AND FOUND

Sandy has been searching all over for Krispy Bear. Help Sandy reunite with her favorite toy!

MESSAGE OF HOPE

Guy wants to lead the Croods family to safety. He's written directions on a boulder. Use the key to decode the message and write the letters on the dashes below.

 =A  =N

=B =O

=C =P

=D =Q

=E =R

=F =S

=G =T

=H =U

=I =V

=J =W

=K =X

=L =Y

=M =Z

W E A D

F O R

T H E

M O U N T A I N

Guy and Grug have a lot of differences. So do these two pictures. Find the 7 differences and bring a little peace to the Croods Brood.

EVOLUTION ERROR

Two of the Mousephants below are identical. The rest are all different. Can you find the two that match?

HUNGRY HYBRID HERBIVORE

The giant Girelephant sees his favorite food across a field of plants. Follow the pattern of perennials down, left, and right (but not diagonally) and help the hungry herbivore reach the tasty veggie.

Follow this pattern!

FLICKERING FIRELIGHT

The shadows of Croods and Creatures flicker across the walls of the cave. Somehow the shadows have become separated from their owners. Can you match them up? One of the characters is not casting a shadow—who is it? Look closely! Circle your answer.

Draw a line from each shadow to its owner.

COUNTIMALS!

Croodaceous creatures are running wild! Follow the
animal key to the right and find all the Creatures
below. Look closely, but don't get too close!

Eep sees something new. What do you see? Look closely and you'll see 7 differences between the two pictures.

The Croods have tumbled off a cliff to a new world. Help Grug make sense of this new world by finding where the six close-up pieces fit into the big picture. Draw a line from each close-up to its place in the scene.

STAY TOGETHER!

The Croods are trying to stay together as they run, but they've lost sight of someone. Can you help? The missing someone is two spaces below Sandy, one space above Grug and next to the Fishcat. Who is it?

JOIN THE HUNT

Sandy wants to help the family hunt for food everyday. Now she needs your help hunting for words that describe her world. Look up, down and diagonally, too!

```
W  T  O  G  R  E  I  G  W  A  C  H  A  F  B
E  J  C  U  R  Y  V  E  V  I  V  R  U  S  B
H  E  L  N  L  R  W  O  R  O  Q  Y  V  N  D
A  E  V  I  I  Y  R  O  L  C  H  A  S  E  T
S  X  M  A  P  T  T  R  S  U  A  K  S  R  W
R  A  C  X  C  S  X  X  J  R  T  T  J  I  T
F  E  U  Y  I  T  D  E  I  G  O  I  Z  F  R
S  T  F  H  P  O  K  K  Z  R  O  K  O  A  I
U  F  E  N  Q  M  D  L  I  W  C  K  E  N  B
N  R  F  A  U  O  U  E  T  O  P  R  E  Y  E
P  G  K  M  A  R  S  D  R  H  E  H  R  W  Z
K  A  Z  E  L  R  S  H  A  B  C  T  Z  G  N
Q  C  Y  V  Q  O  D  O  E  O  U  L  C  E  C
E  D  L  A  G  W  W  N  A  K  E  Z  F  S  E
O  Z  C  C  W  Y  C  A  R  N  I  V  O  R  E
```

SUN	PREY	RULES	CAVEMAN
WILD	HUNT	FAMILY	TOMORROW
CAVE	CHASE	STORIES	CARNIVORE
FIRE	GRRRR	SURVIVE	EVOLUTION
ROCK	TRIBE	EXTINCT	PREHISTORIC

The Croods are on the move! They stay close together by calling out to each other. Who is calling who? Find out by unscrambling each name and writing it below the scrambled version! Here is a key to help you:

Eep   Guy   Gran   Thunk   Sandy   Ugga   Grug

RNAG
Gran

NSYAD
Sandy

UKNHT
Thunk

AGUG
Ugga

FIRED UP

Find the right vine (1, 2, or 3) to get to the Guy's flaming torch. Get fired-up tree hugger!

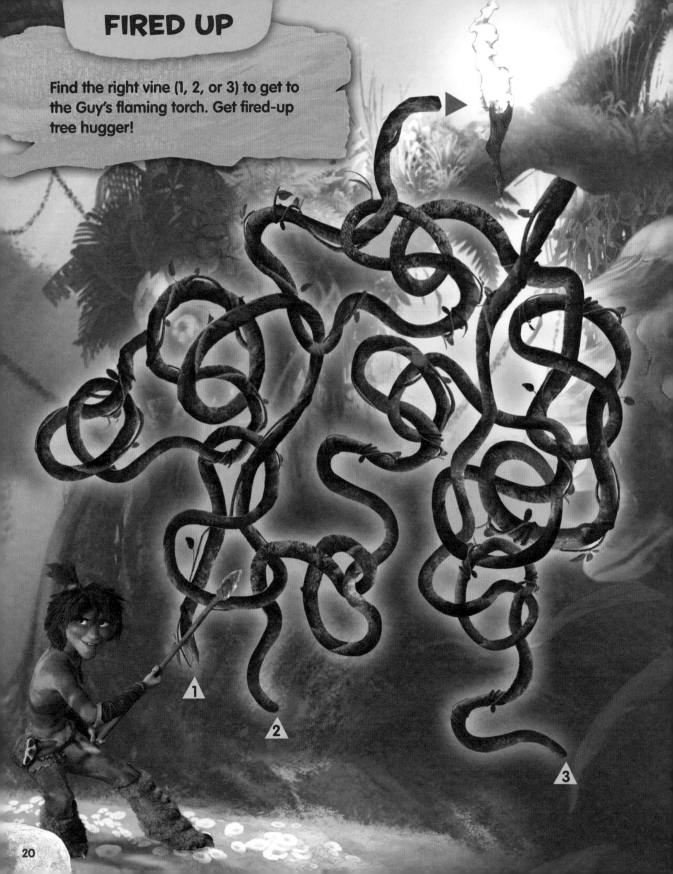

WHAT IN THE WHIRLED?

The Croods' world has gone crazy! Everything safe and routine has been twisted into something new—even cave paintings! See if you can match the whirls to the pictures below. Draw a line from each twisted image to its match below.

This Punch Monkey doesn't care that there are 7 ways these two pictures differ. See if you can find them all. Then, tell the Punch Monkey and RUN!

FIRST COME, FIRST EAT

The competition for food is a day-to-day struggle in the Croods' prehistoric world. The Ramu and the Mousephant are both hungry for the corn at the center of the maze. Who will get there first?

FOUR-SIDED ROUND-UP

Take a close look at the geometric drawing. How many squares can you find? Remember, the four sides of a square are all the same length.

BONUS

How many triangles can you find?

CROOD AWAKENING

Look in the word list to find the best word to finish each sentence.

Crocopup   Douglas   Fishcat   idea   maze

right   sun   swamp   tired   tomorrow

1. Guy plans to hitch a ride on a new _____.

2. Eep believes in _____.

3. The family has to find their way through a _____.

4. Thunk has an unusual name for his pet Crocopup: _____.

5. Grug begins to think that Guy may be _____.

WHO IS THIS GUY?

The Croods had never met anyone like Guy. He seemed to be the complete opposite of Grug. But once they found each other, they stuck together. Find the words in the puzzle below that apply to Guy.

```
H  I  G  H  G  R  O  U  N  D  M  T  R  Y  E
R  E  L  L  E  T  Y  R  O  T  S  H  I  C  V
Y  T  M  R  B  R  Q  R  I  R  U  I  S  X  J
S  N  P  O  E  R  E  O  T  N  O  N  K  T  X
K  F  I  D  S  G  A  N  X  I  R  K  Y  M  W
X  Y  A  A  N  D  G  V  G  A  P  E  V  H  D
Z  E  V  A  R  M  N  W  E  T  H  R  U  B  S
L  S  R  X  V  B  I  A  S  N  S  S  F  M  T
F  T  L  E  B  C  D  W  H  U  I  N  A  R  D
S  U  R  V  I  V  O  R  S  O  H  R  A  M  N
G  R  M  P  N  D  Z  J  E  M  T  P  Q  O  E
Z  X  H  Y  C  E  F  A  C  A  P  G  U  Y  I
P  P  C  L  I  M  W  Q  O  E  M  H  F  W  R
T  D  J  M  C  T  B  H  R  G  S  E  V  A  F
R  E  T  R  A  T  S  E  R  I  F  S  R  K  I
```

GUY	RISKY	DREAMER	STRANGER
NEW	SMART	THINKER	SURVIVOR
BELT	BRAINY	TRAPPER	HIGH GROUND
SWIM	FRIEND	HANDSOME	FIRE STARTER
BRAVE	LEADER	MOUNTAIN	STORYTELLER

CAVE PAINTING

Eep and her family know what it takes to survive in the Croodaceous world. Check out the message she's painted on the wall. Use the key to decode the message and write the letters on the dashes below.

=A   =N
=B   =O
=C   =P
=D   =Q
=E   =R
=F   =S
=G   =T
=H   =U
=I   =V
=J   =W
=K   =X
=L   =Y
=M   =Z

DON'T

MESS

WITH

MY

TRIBE

LONG SHADOWS

The setting sun has cast long—and wrong—shadows behind the cavemen and creatures along the bottom of the page. See if you can pair the shadows with their owners. One character is not casting a shadow. Which one is it? Circle your answer.

Draw a line from each shadow to its owner.

HIDING IN PLAIN SIGHT

The family is trying Grug's new idea—mobile home rocks! Unfortunately, they're not good for hiding. Seven differences between the two pictures are also hiding in plain sight. Find them all!

FETCH, DOUGLAS!

Thunk wants his pet Crocopup to fetch the stick. But to get through the maze, he has to follow the pattern on the right no matter which way it goes. Ready? Go fetch!

Follow this pattern!

34

ROCKIN' RIOT

Grug threatens to rock the riot in a big way. See if you can sort out who's who and count them up. Compare your answers to the key on the right.

3   5   3

4   2   2

The Croods are safely asleep in their cave but Bear Pear sees something strange. Only one of the six close-ups actually matches the picture. Which one is it?

RAMU RUN

Keep an eye out for Ramus. If you see one—run! While you're waiting, look carefully at the pictures below and find the two that look exactly alike.

RACE UP THE ROCK WALL

Show Guy the way to the top of the rock wall by following the pattern of rocks on the right. Start at the green arrow and end at the red arrow. Keep moving!

Follow this pattern!

PREDATOR AND PREY

Thunk wants to join his mother and sister. To reach them, he has to avoid the predators along the way. Can you help Thunk reach his goal without becoming prey?

PREHISTORIC WILDLIFE

Thankfully, the fearsome beasts of the Croodaceous Period have been extinct for eons. Search the puzzle below for the names and characteristics of these yester-zoic creatures!

```
T E E M R Z D C S G R W V J M
M A X C O O H Y N I A V P O A
R A B T R N A D R M M P U A Z
F L C O I E K R O L U S P X G
U W A A R N I E H L E X O F O
R O D G W K C F Y P F F C F L
R R F C N N C T H H M I O L W
Y A H Y H Q I A A A T S R A C
H E F M L U N V J S B H C D L
P B T N A T P S O T J C S I A
E R O V I B R E H R O A S R W
Y R A C S P M F F T E T Z B S
P P U N C H M O N K E Y V Y R
U L I Y O T E H P S V E Y H L
B P R E D A T O R O U W T X Y
```

ROAR	TEETH	BEAR OWL	HERBIVORE
RAMU	HORNS	EXTINCT	JACKROBAT
CLAWS	FIERCE	FISHCAT	MOUSEPHANT
FURRY	HYBRID	CROCOPUP	MACAWNIVORE
SCARY	LIYOTE	PREDATOR	PUNCH MONKEY

ARE WE THERE YET?

As the world's first road trip dragged on, Gran got a little cranky. See if you can crack the code and find out what she needed to feel better. Use the key to decode the message and write the letters on the dashes below.

 =A    =N

=A   =N
=B   =O
=C   =P
=D   =Q
=E   =R
=F   =S
=G   =T
=H   =U
=I   =V
=J   =W
=K   =X
=L   =Y
=M   =Z

I

N E E D

A

S N A C K

42

SPIN-STERS

Who knew cavemen invented spin art? Use your imagination to unspin the characters and match them to the pictures below. Draw a line from each twisted image to its match below.

The Croods don't know what lies ahead, but they do know their world has changed forever. One of these pictures has changed, too, in 7 different ways. Can you spot them all?

PLAYGROUND HUNT

Thunk and Sandy are having a blast in this prehistoric playground. See the items on the right? Several copies of each one are hidden in the picture. Try to find them all!

FAST FOOD

The Macawnivore wants to make a meal out of Guy and the Croods! Their only hope is to lose him in the maze. Show them the way through and save them from being a fast food feast!

GUY TO GUY

All these pictures of Guy may look the same, but only two of them match. Find them!

PREHISTORIC JUMBLE

Take a look at the cave dwellers and critters on the right. The numbers you see are how many of them are hidden in the picture. Can you find them all?

MOUSEPHANT MARCH

How did the Mousephant get from one side of the cave to the other? Follow his footprint 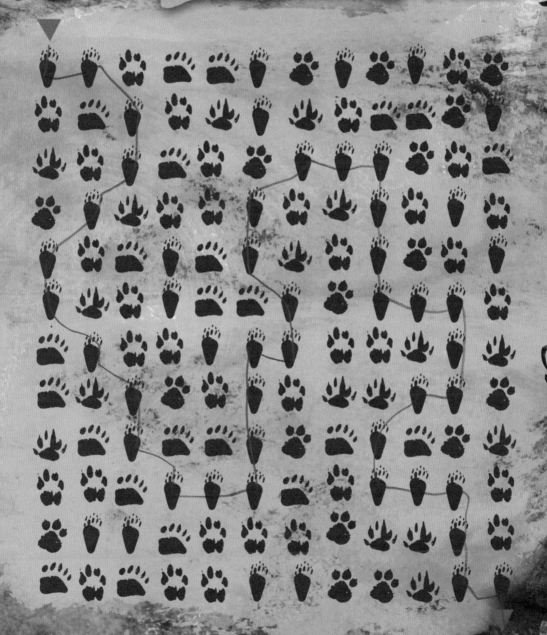 up, down and diagonally to find out!

Grug, Sandy and Gran made a new discovery – popcorn! Picture kernels from the scene are scattered below. See if you can discover where they fit into the jumbo-sized picture. And, pass the butter!

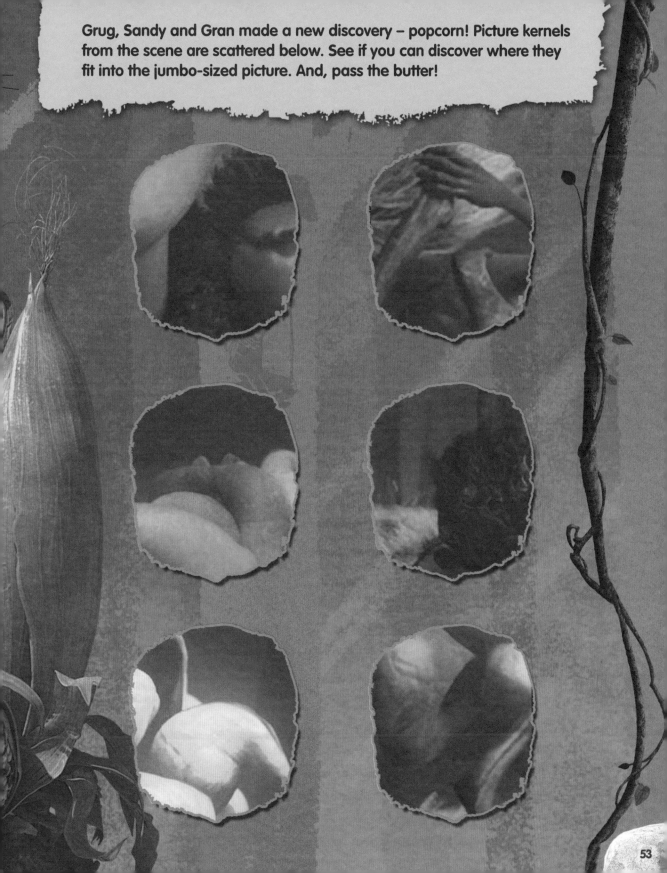

TALES OF TOMORROW

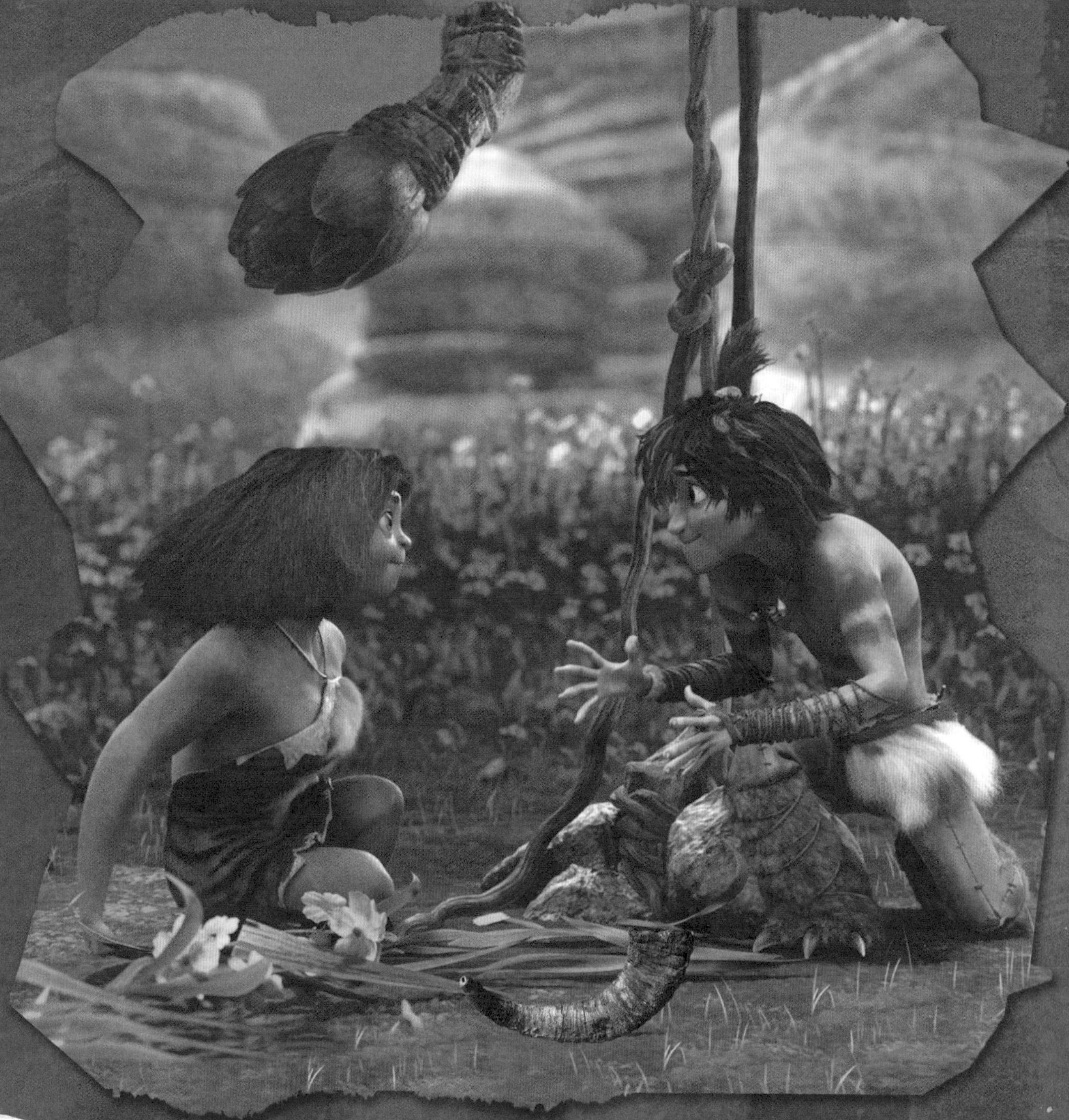

Eep has never met anyone like Guy before. He's so different! These pictures are different, too. In 7 ways, to be exact. See if you can find them all.

TRI-TRIP GERBILS

Count up all the triangles you can find in this geometric design. Look carefully—some are big, some are small. And don't let those pesky Trip Gerbils trip you up!

EVERY DAY THE SAME

Find the best word below to complete each sentence.

belts   cave   fire   hunt   knots

Krispy Bear   lake   new   snore   story

1. Grug likes the safety of the _____.

2. The whole family helps _____.

3. Eep likes Guy. He has _____ ideas.

4. Guy shows the Croods how to make _____.

5. Each night, Grug tells the family a _____.

HITCHIN' A RIDE

Gran's hitching a ride with Thunk as they head for the high ground. Look carefully and see if you can find the two pictures that match. Hang on, Gran!

SCRAMBLED EGGS

Images of cavemen and critters are scrambled up behind the giant eggs, each one with a duplicate. Look behind all the eggs, then close the panels and use your memory to find all six matching pictures!

LAVA LABYRINTH

The Croodaceous Period is coming to a fiery end. Earthquakes and hot lava are ripping the Earth apart. Help Grug tiptoe across the logs to safety!

SCARY SPECIES

ARBE APRE

____ ____

PTIR SLERBGI

____ _____

KROJATCBA

_____

NMWCAAROVEI

_____

URMA

____

These creatures definitely missed a link in the gene pool! Unscramble the names in this mutant mash up, then writing them below the scrambled versions! Then, RUN! Here is a key to help you:

Bear Pear | Trip Gerbils | Punch Monkey | Belt | Jackrobat
Mousephant | Bear Owl | Macawnivore | Ramu | Crocopup

LETB

_ _ _ _

HCUPN EMKOYN

_ _ _ _ _   _ _ _ _ _ _

EHAPUMOTSN

_ _ _ _ _ _ _ _ _ _

AREB LWO

_ _ _ _   _ _ _

PCORCPOU

_ _ _ _ _ _ _ _

Eep watches Grug and Thunk go off to hunt. She wants to join them, but Grug says she's grounded. All Eep can do is work with you to find 7 differences between the two pictures.

SANDY'S SPECIAL FRIEND

Sandy has a special friend. Do you know who it is? Use the key to decode the message and write the letters on the dashes below.

=A =N

=B =O

=C =P

=D =Q

=E =R

=F =S

=G =T

=H =U

=I =V

=J =W

=K =X

=L =Y

=M =Z

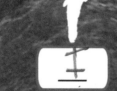

I

LOVE

KRISPY

BEAR

66

BIG PILE OF CROOD

The Croods are all piled up. Pull them apart one at a time and see who's there. Check out the key on the right and find the correct number of each of the Croods.

NOT A PLAY THING!

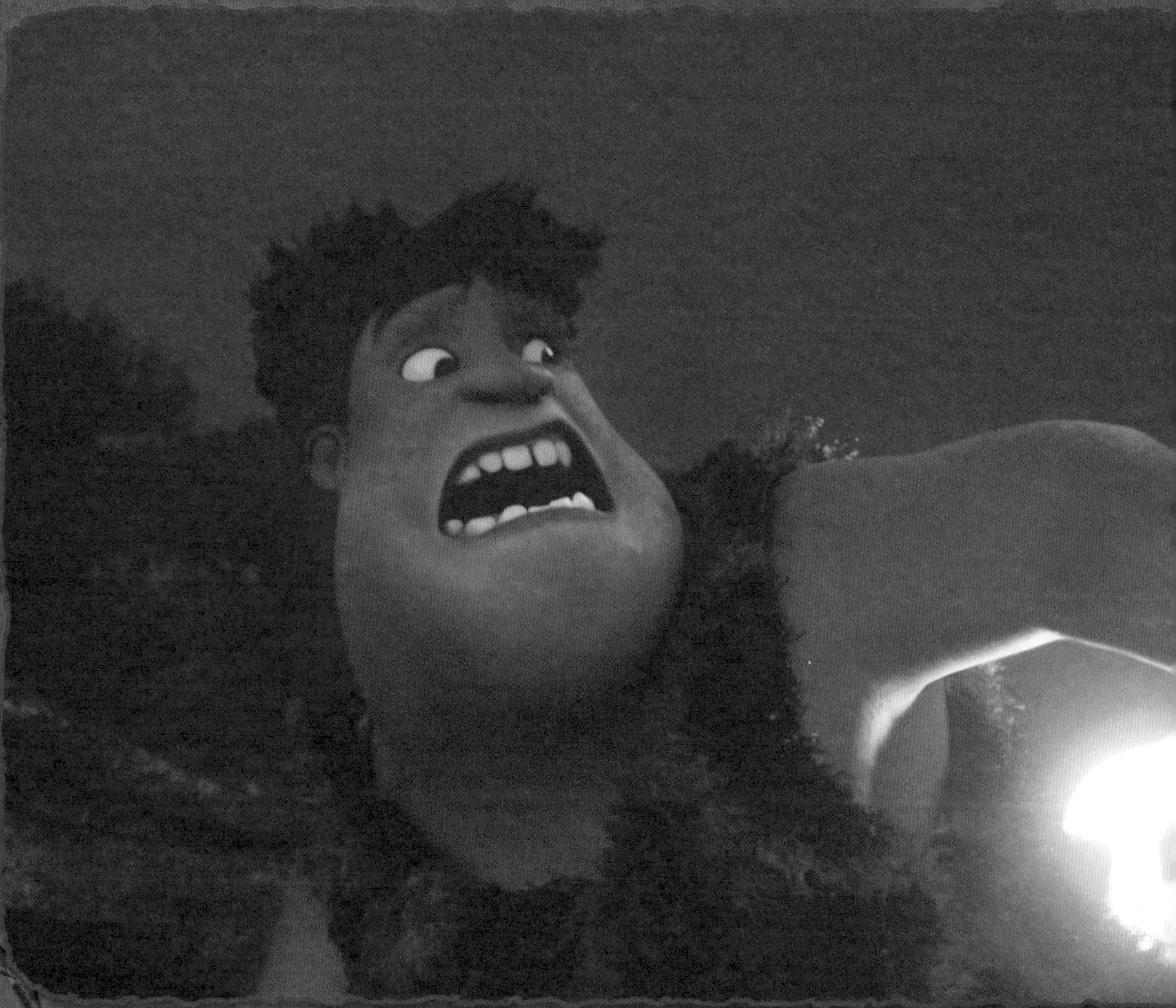

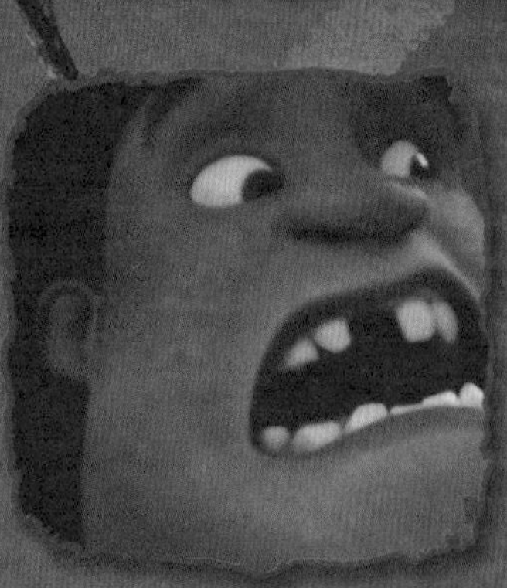

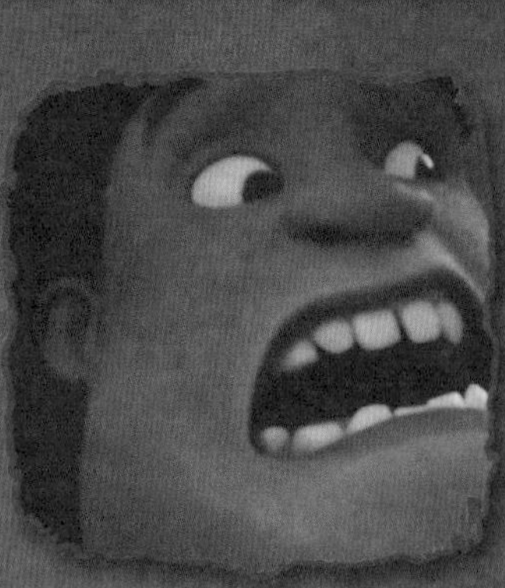

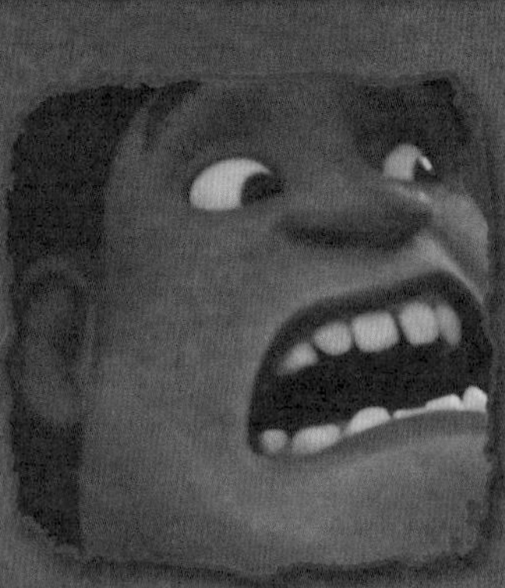

Thunk found out the hard way that fire can "bite"! But it shouldn't be too hard for you to find out which close-ups below fits correctly into the left and right sides of the big picture. Hurry, before Thunk turns the page to ashes!

WHO'D A THUNK IT?

Thunk and his family were forced to find a new place to live when their world was destroyed. Search the puzzle to find words that describe the family and their adventure!

```
C R T U G G A R X T C Z G L U
R L E R N G Y D Q R X C A Q S
A V I T I U A L C T F N G T R
Z C T F S B R Q M V D U V R O
Y U V L F A A I S S R E Q O E
F M M V Y H S L L G G A S A T
V C U Y T P A I Y U G R Y D E
B R U T A L D N D F O T C T M
U I W V P E C S G N E H C R T
C I R A B R A B A E F Q N I H
W B Z J W N K C P P R U A P Z
N Y W T D Y L N V Y T A R R V
W P J Y A O H H U T W K G E Q
U N Z E V R Y Y Z H S E O H S
N Y Q C T Q V B L Z T O O D W
```

EEP	UGGA	BRUTAL	DISASTER
GUY	CRAZY	TRIBAL	ROAD TRIP
RUN	SANDY	METEORS	LANDSLIDE
GRAN	SHOES	VOLCANO	EARTHQUAKE
GRUG	THUNK	BARBARIC	CLIFFHANGER

HEARTY, NOT SMARTY

Take a look at this group of cavemen and mammals. Which one of them is known for having a big heart but not much brainpower? The answer is three spaces below Krispy Bear and three spaces left of the Bear Pear. Good luck!

BARREN AND BLEAK

It looks bleak, but in this landscape is a garden of prehistoric plants. They're pictured on the right. The numbers show how many are hidden in the picture. Find them all!

SCARY SHADOWS

Scary shadows dance across the walls of the cave. But they're not so scary when you know who it really is. Match the shadows to their owners! Which one is not making a shadow? Circle your answer!

Draw a line from each shadow to its owner.

ANSWERS

PAGES 2-3

4 ⬇ 2 ⬇ 3 ⬇ 6 ⬇ 4 ⬇ 2 ⬇

PAGE 4

PAGE 5

Head for the mountain.

PAGES 6-7

PAGE 8

PAGE 9

PAGE 10

PAGE 11

4 — 2 — 2
4 — 3 — 5

PAGES 12-13

PAGES 14-15

PAGE 16

PAGE 17

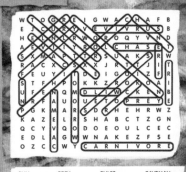

SUN | PREY | RULES | CAVEMAN
WILD | HUNT | FAMILY | TOMORROW
CAVE | CHASE | STORIES | CARNIVORE
FIRE | GRRRR | SURVIVE | EVOLUTION
ROCK | TRIBE | EXTINCT | PREHISTORIC

PAGES 18-19

Eep

Gran

Guy

Grug

Thunk

Sandy

Ugga

PAGE 20

PAGE 21

PAGES 22-23

76

PAGE 24

PAGE 25

18 squares
28 triangles

PAGE 26

1. Guy plans to hitch a ride on a new **sun**.
2. Eep believes in **tomorrow**.
3. The family has to find their way through a **maze**.
4. Thunk has an unusual name for his pet crocopup: **Douglas**.
5. Grug begins to think that Guy may be **right**.

PAGE 27

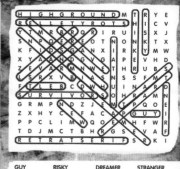

GUY	RISKY	DREAMER	STRANGER
NEW	SMART	THINKER	SURVIVOR
BELT	BRAINY	TRAPPER	HIGH GROUND
SWIM	FRIEND	HANDSOME	FIRE STARTER
BRAVE	LEADER	MOUNTAIN	STORYTELLER

PAGE 28 Don't mess with my tribe.

PAGE 31

PAGES 32-33

PAGE 34

PAGE 35

3 5 3
4 2 2

PAGES 36-37

PAGE 38

77

PAGE 39

PAGE 40

PAGE 41

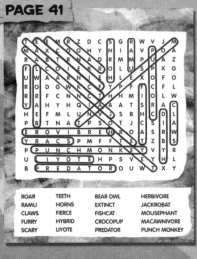

ROAR
RAMU
CLAWS
FURRY
SCARY

TEETH
HORNS
FIERCE
HYBRID
LIYOTE

BEAR OWL
EXTINCT
FISHCAT
CROCOPUP
PREDATOR

HERBIVORE
JACKROBAT
MOUSEPHANT
MACAWNIVORE
PUNCH MONKEY

PAGE 42   I need a snack!

PAGE 43

PAGES 44-45

PAGE 48

PAGES 46-47

3 4 2 6 3 5

PAGE 49

78

PAGE 50

5 2 3
3 4 2

PAGE 51

PAGES 52-53

3
1   6
5   2
4

1 2
3 4
5 6

PAGES 54-55

PAGE 56

37 triangles

PAGE 57

1. Grug likes the safety of the <u>cave</u>.
2. The whole family helps **hunt**.
3. Eep likes Guy. He has **<u>new</u>** ideas.
4. Guy shows the Croods how to make **<u>fire</u>**.
5. Each night, Grug tells the family a **<u>story</u>**.

PAGE 58

PAGE 61

PAGES 62-63

Bear Pear
Trip Gerbils
Jackrobat
Punch Monkey
Belt
Mousephant
Macawnivore
Bear Owl
Ramu
Crocopup

PAGES 64-65

PAGE 66 I love Krispy Bear.

PAGE 67

PAGE 70

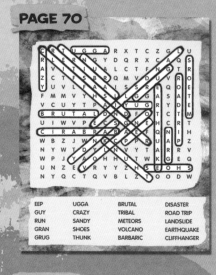

EEP   UGGA   BRUTAL   DISASTER
GUY   CRAZY   TRIBAL   ROAD TRIP
RUN   SANDY   METEORS   LANDSLIDE
GRAN   SHOES   VOLCANO   EARTHQUAKE
GRUG   THUNK   BARBARIC   CLIFFHANGER

PAGES 68-69

PAGE 71

PAGES 72-73

PAGE 74